CONTENTS

Meet the TARDIS

Introduction...................................4
TARDIS Data..................................6
TARDIS Anatomy 8
⬢ Test your knowledge

TARDIS Travellers

The Doctor...................................10
Martha...11
Donna..11
Captain Jack................................12
Rose...13
⬢ Test your knowledge

TARDIS Enemies

The Reapers.................................14
The Sycorax.................................14
The Daleks...................................15
The Family of Blood.....................16
The Weeping Angels....................16
The Master...................................17
⬢ Test your knowledge

TARDIS Origins

Gallifrey.......................................18
The Time Lords............................20
⬢ Test your knowledge

Transport and Technology

Time and space travel..................22
The Chameleon circuit.................24
Translator.....................................25
⬢ Test your knowledge

Adventures in Time and Space

The Parting of the Ways..............26
The Runaway Bride.......................27
Human Nature/The Family of Blood.........28
Utopia..29
⬢ Test your knowledge

Test your knowledge Answers 30

The Secret of the Stones...........31

MEET THE TARDIS

The TARDIS might look like an old police telephone box, but the unassuming blue wooden box hides so much more. It's a spaceship. It's a time machine. It's the Doctor's home and his best friend.

The initials stand for Time And Relative Dimension In Space. It can dematerialise in one place and materialise in any time or on any planet that the Doctor chooses. Sometimes, the TARDIS chooses for him and leads him into all kinds of adventures! The first thing the Doctor's companions notice about the TARDIS is that it's much bigger on the inside than the outside. It's because it uses amazing Time Lord technology that makes it dimensionally transcendental. It was quite a shock to Martha, but she soon got used to it and settled down for the ride of a lifetime.

POLICE PUBLIC CALL BOX

POLICE TELEPHONE
FREE
FOR USE OF
PUBLIC
ADVICE & ASSISTANCE
OBTAINABLE IMMEDIATELY
OFFICER & CARS
RESPOND TO ALL CALLS
PULL TO OPEN

The TARDIS contains any number of rooms and everything the Doctor might ever need is stored inside. When he regenerated into his tenth body, he searched through the vast wardrobe to find a suitable outfit for his new personality. This huge store of clothes is especially useful when visiting historical times, as it allows the Doctor and his companions to dress up and blend in with the locals, without attracting too much attention in their 21st century clothes! The Doctor even managed to produce a scooter from somewhere deep within the TARDIS, when he and Rose visited the 1950s.

Name: TARDIS, which stands for Time And Relative Dimension in Space

Age: Over 900 years old, like the Doctor

Owner: The Doctor

Size: The TARDIS is bigger on the inside than the outside!

Current Appearance: 1950s police telephone box

POLICE PUBLIC CALL BOX

POLICE TELEPHONE
FREE
FOR USE OF
PUBLIC
ADVICE & ASSISTANCE
OBTAINABLE IMMEDIATELY
OFFICER & CARS
RESPOND TO ALL CALLS
PULL TO OPEN

POLICE PUBLIC CALL BOX

Glass column contains the Time Rotor, which lights up and moves when the TARDIS is in flight

TARDIS console

Emergency hammer

1. WHAT DOES TARDIS STAND FOR?
A. Take A Ride Down Inverness Street
B. Time And Relative Dimension in Space
C. Tell Aliens Rose Died in Scotland

2. HOW OLD IS THE TARDIS?
A. Over 900 years
B. 92 years
C. It's brand new

3. WHERE IS THE TIME ROTOR?
A. In the glass column on the console
B. In the Doctor's pocket
C. On Earth

4. WHAT DOES THE TARDIS LOOK LIKE?
A. A police telephone box
B. A large rock
C. A sweet shop

P

Seats for bumpy rides

THE DOCTOR

After the Doctor survived the Great Time War, the TARDIS was one of the few things that remained of his destroyed home planet, Gallifrey. The TARDIS is the Doctor's best friend - after all, they've been travelling together for hundreds of years. She has accompanied him through many adventures and several different bodies! The TARDIS is an important part of the Doctor's ability to regenerate and he couldn't survive without her. One of the worst moments of the Doctor's long life was watching the TARDIS doors close as his ancient enemy the Master stole her from him.

5. WHAT TYPE OF SHIP IS
   THE TARDIS?
A. A Type 19 Rocket
B. A Type 33 Saucer
C. A Type 40 TT Capsule

TEST YOUR
KNOWLEDGE

MARTHA

Martha's first impression of the TARDIS was just like every other human's who has entered it - she couldn't believe it was really bigger on the inside! She was surprised to see that the TARDIS has no crew and the Doctor travels alone. She soon got used to the idea though, and loves travelling through time and space with the Doctor.

DONNA

Donna was very surprised to find herself in the TARDIS! She'd been filled with Huon energy as part of an alien plot. The heart of the TARDIS also contains Huon Particles, and the two sets of Particles magnetised to pull Donna into the TARDIS. She thought she'd been abducted by a Martian, but the Doctor helped her escape from the real alien threat, the Empress of the Racnoss.

CAPTAIN JACK HARKNESS

Captain Jack's travels in the TARDIS began when he met the Doctor during World War II and his own spaceship was destroyed. When Rose used the Time Vortex to bring him back to life after he was killed by the Daleks, he was left behind on the Game Station and thought he'd never see the Doctor again. The Time Vortex made Jack indestructible and he made his way back to Earth and waited over 100 years for the Doctor to return for him. When he finally heard the grinding of the ancient engines, he hitched a ride on the outside of the TARDIS to the year one hundred trillion - the end of the universe - and helped the Doctor and Martha to defeat the Master.

ROSE

Only Rose's connection to the TARDIS comes anywhere close to the Doctor's. When he thought her life was in danger on the Game Station, he used the TARDIS to send her home. But Rose couldn't leave him and she forced the TARDIS console open. The Time Vortex inside flowed into her, taking her back to the Doctor and allowing her to see all of time and space. She destroyed the Daleks and their Emperor. But the energy of the Vortex was killing her, so the Doctor took it into himself to save her, which caused him to regenerate.

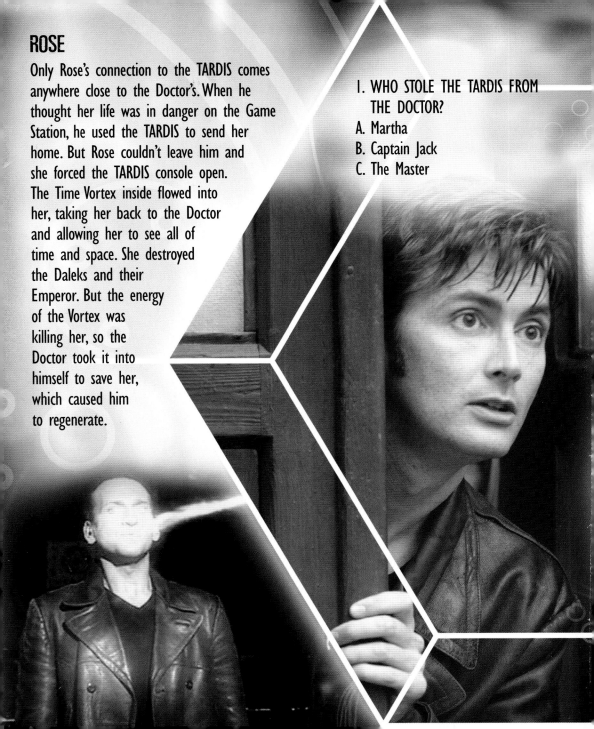

1. WHO STOLE THE TARDIS FROM THE DOCTOR?
A. Martha
B. Captain Jack
C. The Master

THE REAPERS

When Rose created a paradox in time by going into the past and saving her dad's life, the TARDIS suffered. The Doctor opened the doors to discover it had turned into an empty wooden box. Only when Pete Tyler died as he should have, did the TARDIS return to normal.

THE SYCORAX

While the Tenth Doctor was recovering from his regeneration, the Sycorax teleported the TARDIS, along with Rose and members of the British government on to their ship. The TARDIS protected the unconscious Doctor from the alien invaders, but its translation circuits couldn't operate while the Doctor slept.

2. WHEN DID CAPTAIN JACK MEET THE DOCTOR?
A. During World War II
B. Last Tuesday
C. Christmas Day

3. WHICH PART OF THE TARDIS DID ROSE BREAK OPEN?
A. The doors
B. The console
C. The telephone

4. WHAT PULLED DONNA INTO THE TARDIS?
A. Huon particles
B. The Doctor
C. Martians

5. WHAT COULDN'T THE DOCTOR DO WITHOUT THE TARDIS?
A. Cook
B. Survive
C. Knit

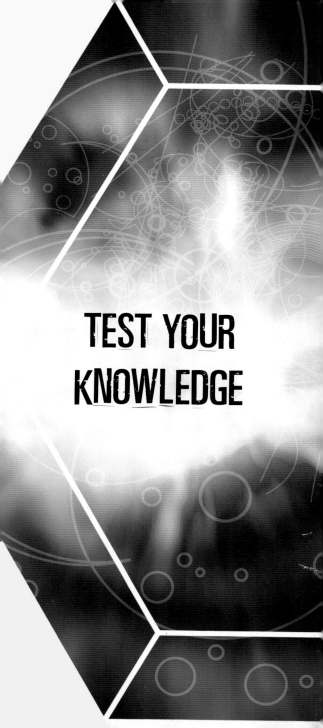

TEST YOUR
KNOWLEDGE

THE DALEKS

Any enemy of the Doctor's is an enemy of the TARDIS, and the Daleks are one of his greatest foes. He's come up against them many times, but it's not often they actually make it inside the TARDIS! When the Daleks captured Rose on the Game Station, Captain Jack and the Doctor were so quick to rush to her rescue that they materialised the TARDIS around a Dalek, as well as Rose. Jack destroyed the lone Dalek with his defabricator and they used the Slitheen extrapolator to protect themselves and the TARDIS from the remaining Daleks. Rose was able to use the powers of the heart of the TARDIS to destroy the Daleks and their Emperor.

THE FAMILY OF BLOOD

The Family of Blood used a stolen Time Agent's Vortex Manipulator to track the Doctor and his TARDIS through time and space. The Doctor was able to put the TARDIS on emergency power to hide itself from them, while he hid his own identity in a Time Lord pocket watch. The Family wanted his Gallifreyan life force to help them live forever.

THE WEEPING ANGELS

The Weeping Angels sent the Doctor and Martha back into the past, then stole his TARDIS. They wanted to feast on the time energy inside, but they couldn't open the doors without the key. Sally Sparrow helped to return the TARDIS to the Doctor and turn the Angels to stone, before they could do any damage.

5. WHERE WAS THE MASTER'S
   IDENTITY HIDDEN?
A. The TARDIS
B. A pocket watch
C. Down the back of the sofa

TEST YOUR
KNOWLEDGE

THE POWER OF THE TIME LORDS

Centuries ago, during what the Time Lords call 'The Old Time', Rassilon, their greatest leader, discovered the secret of space-time travel. But to make it a reality he needed a huge source of power. He worked with a stellar engineer called Omega to try to harness the energy of a black hole. Omega used a stellar manipulator sometimes known as The Hand of Omega to turn the black hole into a source of unimaginable power.

Omega was lost in the resulting supernova, but Rassilon managed to control the nucleus of the black hole. Each TARDIS carried a direct link to this power source, which Rassilon called The Eye of Harmony.

POLICE PUBLIC CALL BOX

POLICE PUBLIC CALL BOX

POLICE TELEPHONE
FREE
FOR USE OF
PUBLIC
ADVICE & ASSISTANCE
OBTAINABLE IMMEDIATELY
OFFICER & CARS
RESPOND TO ALL CALLS
PULL TO OPEN

THE MASTER

The Doctor thought his oldest enemy, the Master, had died in the Great Time War along with the rest of the Time Lords. When the Face of Boe said to him "You are not alone.", the last thing the Doctor expected was that the Master had survived. He was living in the far distant future, using the Time Lord technique of hiding his alien identity in a very special pocket watch. He was unaware of his true identity until the Doctor arrived. The Master once had a TARDIS of his own, but had to steal the Doctor's to escape from the planet Malcassairo.

1. WHICH REGENERATION OF THE DOCTOR'S MET THE SYCORAX?
A. Eighth
B. Ninth
C. Tenth

2. WHAT DIDN'T WORK WHEN THE DOCTOR WAS UNCONSCIOUS?
A. Chameleon circuit
B. Translation circuit
C. Sonic screwdriver

3. WHAT DID ROSE USE TO DEFEAT THE DALEKS?
A. The Time Vortex
B. Sonic screwdriver
C. Persuasion

4. WHO SAVED THE TARDIS FROM THE WEEPING ANGELS?
A. Rose
B. Martha
C. Sally Sparrow

THE HEART OF THE TARDIS

The Doctor's TARDIS is actually a Type 40 TT Capsule. The central column of the TARDIS main console, sometimes referred to as the Time Rotor, is the very heart of the machine. The main energy source for the TARDIS is under that column, and held in check by it. When the column moves, it proves the extent of the power thrust. If the column were to come out of the console completely, the power would be free to escape. As Rose discovered — the power at the heart of the TARDIS is the tremendous, deadly power of the Time Vortex itself.

IS THE TARDIS ALIVE?

TARDISes are not built like other machines so much as grown. The actual process remains one of the greatest secrets of the Time Lords. But it raises an interesting question — is the TARDIS in some sense alive?

At times, the Doctor has behaved as if he believes the TARDIS is a living thing and has said as much. While the First Doctor called it his 'ship', the Third Doctor was just as likely to refer to the TARDIS as 'old girl'. We know that the TARDIS has telepathic circuits and has several times seemed to act on its own initiative to save the Doctor...

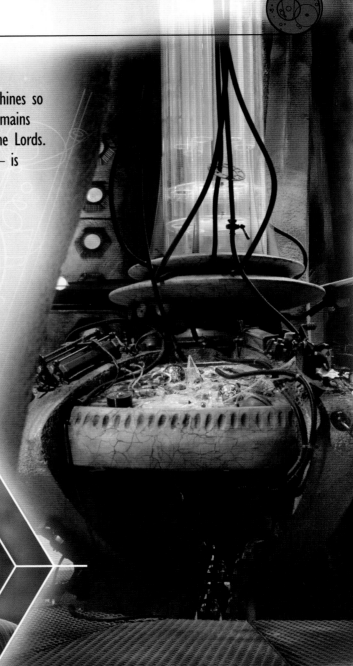

TIME AND SPACE TRAVEL

In theory, the Doctor can programme the flight computer with coordinates and travel to anywhere or anywhen in time and space. Often though, the TARDIS decides for him and takes the Doctor and his companions to wherever they can be the most useful! It usually travels through the Vortex, dematerialising from one place, and materialising in another, but it can also fly conventionally, such as when the Doctor rescued Donna from the Santa Robot taxi driver.

FUEL

Power for the TARDIS comes from the Artron energy in the Eye of Harmony, an artificial black hole created by the Time Lords. However, the Doctor can also park the TARDIS on rifts in time, like the one in Cardiff, to allow it to soak up the radiation.

THE LAST TARDIS?

If the Doctor is the last of the Time Lords, is his TARDIS the last of their time machines? The Doctor has met other rogue Time Lords with stolen TARDISes over the years. A strange meddling monk hoping to help King Harold win the battle of Hastings had a TARDIS that looked identical inside to the Doctor's. The amoral Time Lady the Rani also had her own TARDIS. Like the Doctor, the Master survived the Great Time War, though he seems not to have saved his TARDIS. Over the years he has acquired several — all of them more advanced than the Doctor's. Perhaps somewhere he has another, hidden away and waiting...

1. WHO WAS THE GREATEST LEADER OF THE TIME LORDS?
A. The Master
B. Rassilon
C. Omega

2. WHAT POWER LIES AT THE HEART OF THE TARDIS?
A. The Time Vortex
B. The Time Battery
C. The Rassilon Reactor

3. HOW ARE TARDISES GROWN?
A. In an allotment
B. It's a secret
C. Under water

4. WHAT DID THE THIRD DOCTOR CALL THE TARDIS?
A. Boris
B. His ship
C. Old girl

DIMENSIONALLY TRANSCENDENTAL

The Time Lords developed an incredible technology which allowed them to make things that are much bigger on the inside than they appear on the outside. The inside and the outside somehow exist in two different dimensions, that are connected at the entrance to the TARDIS. This technology was also used to create the Genesis Ark, a capsule that was used to imprison thousands of Daleks during the Great Time War. Even the Doctor's pockets are bigger on the inside!

CHAMELEON CIRCUIT

One of the key features of any TARDIS is its chameleon circuit, which allows it to change shape to blend in to its surroundings wherever it lands. The chameleon circuit on the Doctor's TARDIS has been broken for a long time, trapping it in its disguise as a 1950s police box. The Doctor could fix it if he wanted to, but he's become quite attached to the old blue box.

CHAMELEON ARCH

The chameleon arch allows the Doctor to rewrite every cell in his body, so he can become whoever, or whatever, he wants to be. He used it to disguise himself as a human when hiding from the Family of Blood.

TRANSLATION CIRCUIT

The TARDIS is telepathic and has a translation circuit. It gets into the head of anyone who travels in it, translating alien languages and writing into the traveller's own language. It allows the Doctor and his companions to understand each other and everyone they meet. The translation circuit rarely fails, but it was unable to translate the writing of the Beast on Krop Tor, as it was more ancient than even the TARDIS itself.

1. WHO DID CAPTAIN JACK GET THE EXTRAPOLATOR FROM?
A. The Gelth
B. The Weeping Angels
C. The Slitheen

2. WHAT ALLOWS THE TARDIS TO CHANGE ITS APPEARANCE?
A. Chameleon circuit
B. Spider circuit
C. Hummingbird circuit

3. WHO WAS THE DOCTOR HIDING FROM WHEN HE BECAME HUMAN?
A. The Family of Blood
B. Martha
C. Professor Yana

4. WHAT IS THE EYE OF HARMONY?
A. A telescope
B. An artificial black hole
C. A jewel

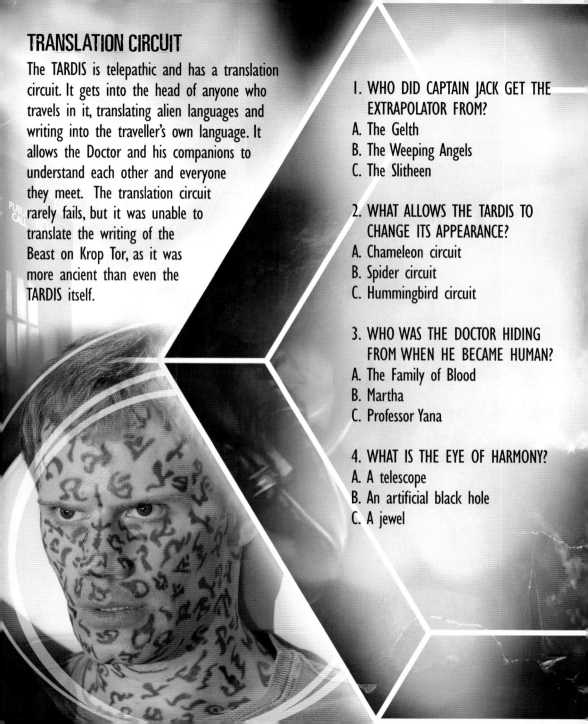

THE PARTING OF THE WAYS

While fighting the Daleks on the Game Station, the Doctor tricked Rose into the TARDIS and sent her back to her own time. On the way, the TARDIS showed Rose a hologram message from the Doctor telling her that his life was in danger and that she would be safer at home. Rose was devastated and enlisted Jackie and Mickey's help to break into the TARDIS console and return to the Doctor's side. Rose looked into the heart of the TARDIS and the Time Vortex flowed into her. She became goddess-like, and was able to delete every atom of the Daleks' existence. But the energy of the Time Vortex was too strong, and for Rose to survive, the Doctor had to take the Vortex into himself and regenerate.

POLICE TELEPHO

FREE

5. WHERE DID THE DOCTOR
   MEET THE BEAST?
A. Krop Tor
B. The supermarket
C. New York

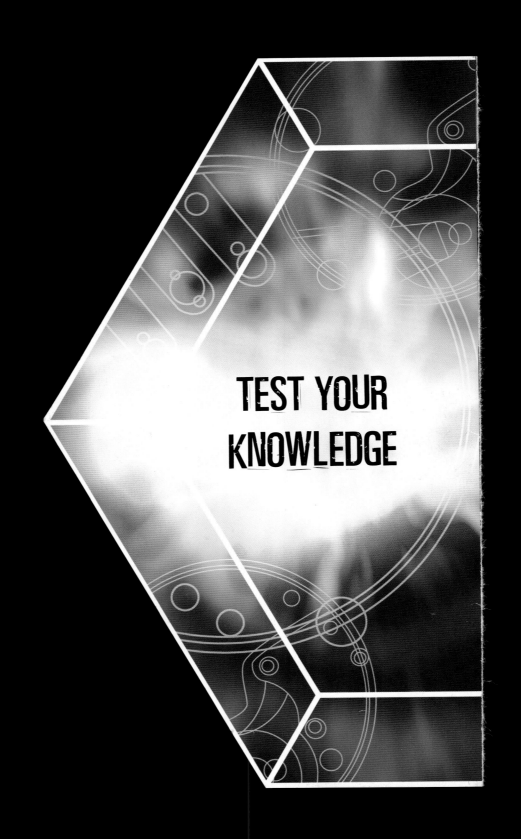

THE RUNAWAY BRIDE

Travelling alone, the Doctor was just as surprised as Donna when she suddenly materialised inside the TARDIS. Donna thought she was being abducted, but the TARDIS was saving her from being part of an alien plot. She had been fed with Huon Particles which magnetised with those in the heart of the TARDIS and pulled her into it. The Empress of the Racnoss wanted to use her as a key to unlock a ship full of young Racnoss hidden at the Earth's core. The Doctor was able to use the Empress' own weapons against her. He flooded her lair and destroyed her plans for world domination.

HUMAN NATURE/THE FAMILY OF BLOOD

When the Family of Blood chased the Doctor across the universe, he used the chameleon arch to turn himself into a human and become a schoolteacher called John Smith. The TARDIS created a whole new life for him and remained hidden in a barn near the school, while Martha became a maid who watched over the Doctor. He left her a message in the TARDIS, with instructions on what to do while the alien part of him was gone. When the Family caught up with them, Martha had to force John Smith to face up to who he really was, and the Doctor returned to defeat them.

5. WHERE WAS PROFESSOR YANA
TRYING TO SEND PEOPLE?
A. Utopia
B. Malcassairo
C. Krop Tor

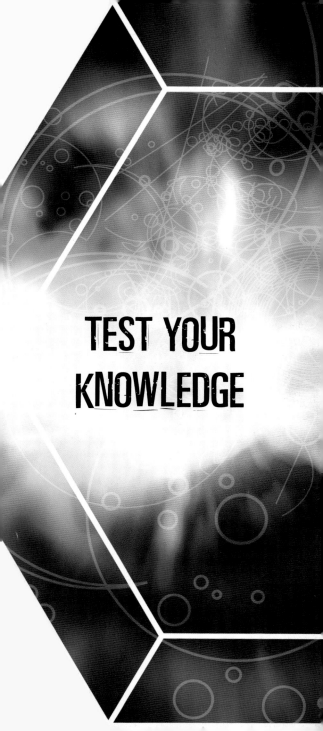
TEST YOUR
KNOWLEDGE

ANSWERS

Meet the TARDIS
1 (b) 2 (a) 3 (a) 4 (a) 5 (b)

TARDIS Travellers
1 (c) 2 (a) 3 (b) 4 (a) 5 (b)

TARDIS Enemies
1 (c) 2 (b) 3 (a) 4 (c) 5 (b)

TARDIS Origins
1 (b) 2 (a) 3 (b) 4 (c) 5 (c)

Transport and Technology
1 (c) 2 (a) 3 (a) 4 (b) 5 (a)

Adventures in Time and Space
1 (a) 2 (b) 3 (c) 4 (c) 5 (a)

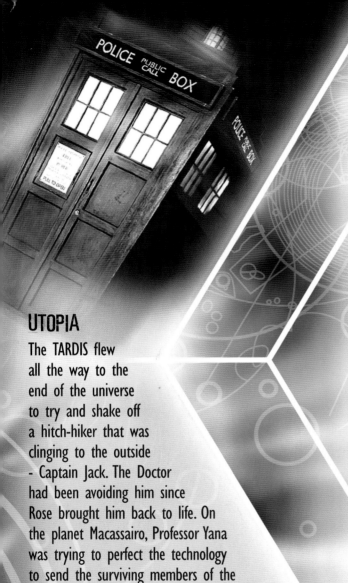

UTOPIA

The TARDIS flew
all the way to the
end of the universe
to try and shake off
a hitch-hiker that was
clinging to the outside
- Captain Jack. The Doctor
had been avoiding him since
Rose brought him back to life. On
the planet Macassairo, Professor Yana
was trying to perfect the technology
to send the surviving members of the
human race to a place called Utopia.
The Doctor was horrified when he realised
Professor Yana was actually his ancient enemy,
the Master. The Master stole the TARDIS and left
the Doctor stranded in a dying universe..

1. WHERE DID THE DOCTOR SEND
   ROSE IN THE TARDIS?
A. Home
B. New Earth
C. Brighton

2. WHAT HAD DONNA BEEN FED WITH?
A. Chips
B. Huon Particles
C. Banana milkshake

3. WHO HITCH-HIKED ON THE SIDE
   OF THE TARDIS?
A. The Master
B. Rose
C. Captain Jack

4. WHAT DID MARTHA WORK
   AS WHILE THE DOCTOR
   WAS HUMAN?
A. A doctor
B. A writer
C. A maid

THE SECRET OF THE STONES

Martha was sitting on one of the chairs close to the main TARDIS console, watching the Doctor as he fiddled with the controls. Because that was what he was doing – fiddling. It was like he didn't trust the TARDIS just to get on with it. Every few seconds he'd click his tongue and turn a control, or press a switch, or move the first control back again to where it had been originally. And while he did it he hummed and tapped his feet.

'There, that should do it.' The Doctor grinned at Martha. But his grin turned into a perplexed look and

he turned back to the controls and changed something else. 'There,' he said again a moment later. 'That should do it.'

'Do what, exactly?' Martha asked. 'I mean, what are you doing? Apart from hopping about like a cat on hot bricks.'

He acted all confused at that. 'Hopping? I don't hop – I glide. Rhythm and style. And why would you put a cat on hot bricks? That's cruel. That's nasty. That's…' He shrugged and sighed as he tried to work out what it was.

'A turn of phrase?' Martha suggested. 'I was just saying. So where are we off to for this little trip?'

'I don't know.'

'But you were… fiddling.'

'Was I? Fiddling? Suppose I was. A bit. Well, maybe not fiddling exactly. Doesn't matter anyway, it's all automatic.' He sniffed and looked suddenly slightly sad. 'I just like to be here. To help.'

Martha laughed 'Help the TARDIS?'

'She's getting on a bit.'

'I sometimes wonder who's in charge here,' Martha said, smiling.

The Doctor raised his eyebrows. 'You'd be surprised.' Before she could ask him what – if anything – he meant by that, he went on: 'So where do you want to go then? What do you want to see? Pick a date, choose a place. Anything.'

'Well, how about – '

'Anything at all. Battle of Waterloo, Charge of the Light Brigade, opening ceremony for the 2116 underwater Olympics. Anything.'

'I was wondering – '

'The moon? No, hang on, done that. Different moon maybe – third moon of Templastagon Five, beautiful sunsets.'

Martha was standing up now, hands on hips. Giving him a look.

'What? Where? Just say. Anywhere. Anywhen.'

'Yeah – if I could get a word in.'

'Mum's the word,' he promised.

'I was just thinking, we've met Shakespeare and solved the mystery of

his lost play and whatever.'

'True.' The Doctor grimaced. 'Sorry.' Put his finger on his lips and nodded for her to go on.

'So, why don't we go and solve some of the other great mysteries of the past?' Martha watched the Doctor, still standing with his finger on his lips. 'And you may answer,' she prompted.

'Thanks, mum. So – history's mysteries? Good thought. Could be fun. Intriguing and exciting. Where do you want to start?'

'I don't know. What about the Mary Celeste? You know, that sailing ship they found drifting deserted like everyone just disappeared.'

The Doctor pulled a face and shook his head. 'Done that.'

'Oh? Going to tell me about it?'

'One day maybe. Look,' he was suddenly earnest and sincere, 'it wasn't my fault, all right?'

'All right, all right. Well, how about the Princes in the Tower, or have you done that too?'

'Twice. Which version of history d'you want?'

'Building the Pyramids?'

'Can't take the credit,' the Doctor admitted modestly. 'Though I know a man who can. I say "man" but actually…'

She didn't let him get any further. 'Stonehenge?'

'Stonehenge? Great big chunks of rock sitting about on Salisbury Plain? What about it?'

'How was it done? How did ancient people get great big chunks of rock there? And why bother anyway? Must have taken them forever.'

'Well, I don't know.' He grinned massively. 'Shall we go and find out?'

The blue box that was the TARDIS floated and spun through

the time vortex, its tough outer shell protecting the Doctor and Martha from the terrible power and energy of the vortex. It dipped and turned, twisted and fell as it headed for its destination – somewhere in time and space…

'The how isn't really all that interesting,' the Doctor decided as he adjusted various controls. There was more purpose

POLICE PUBLIC CALL BOX

POLICE TELEPHONE
FREE
FOR USE OF
PUBLIC
ADVICE & ASSISTANCE
OBTAINABLE IMMEDIATELY
OFFICER & CARS
RESPOND TO ALL CALLS
PULL TO OPEN

in his actions now – less fiddling. 'I mean, bits
of rock stuck in the ground. Not too difficult,
that. Other bits of rock balanced on the bits
of rock in the ground? Not really a problem
if you've got a decent antigravity lift..'

'So, you're keen then?'

'Dead keen. So keen I could hop.' He
paused to demonstrate. 'Because the real
question is – why?'

'Why?'

'Yes, why? Why did they
bother? Apart from the because-we-
can attitude. Because it isn't there,
sort of thing. And maybe – just
maybe – we'll find out what they
thought they were doing. Right,

here we go.' He swept a lever across with a flourish, evidently
pleased with himself.

'Great. I'll get my coat.'

'Excuse me?' School master voice now. 'To observe
is to change.'

'You what?'

'We go blundering about out there while they're deciding
what sort of ancient monument to set up and we could influence
their decision. Don't want to interfere, do we? Sometimes just
watching can change things and we can't be having that.'

'That's a switch,' Martha thought.

'No, so what we do right – and this is the clever bit – we
set the TARDIS to appear just for a few moments, and we take a
snapshot with the scanner. Then after we dematerialise again we
can have a look and see what's going on.'

'Like postcards.'

'Postcards from history, yeah – I like that. Don't know the exact date and we need to see the work in progress, so we'll pop up for a second or two at the same point every year for a few centuries and see how things progress.'

'Time lapse photography,' Martha realised. 'Like how they do those speeded up films of flowers growing. Or buildings being put up.'

'Exactamundo.' The Doctor frowned. 'Maybe not the best word I could have chosen, but anyway…'

While the TARDIS continued with its pre-programmed cycle of appearing and taking snapshots over the years, the Doctor and Martha looked at the first few pictures.

'Fascinating,' the Doctor decided.

'It's a field,' Martha pointed out.

'Well, at the moment it is. Once the Henge-men get going

through. He paged forward through the next few years.

'Still a field.'

'They could do with inventing the lawn mower. Or sheep. Yeah, sheep would sort it out. Given a few years. Look at that grass grow!'

One picture showed a man standing in the long grass. He was dressed in simple clothes made from animal skins and his face was smeared with mud and paint. The Doctor waved to him, though he was only a photo.

'Hi there – thanks for coming. Good job I thought to line the TARDIS up with the rising sun,' he added in a whisper to Martha, as if afraid the man in the picture might hear him. 'He won't have seen us. Probably.'

A few pictures – a few years – later and it got interesting. There were more people on the grassy plain, and the first rocks were arriving – huge megaliths. Enormous lumps of granite being set up in the familiar circular structure.

'Rising sun?' Martha asked.

'Summer solstice in fact.' The Doctor nudged her with his shoulder, his hands deep in his trouser pockets. 'Seemed appropriate.'

On the scanner, Stonehenge rose from Salisbury Plain, complete at last. Or so it seemed to the Doctor and Martha from the view they had. In fact, there was one stone missing, one stone yet to be placed. One very important stone.

Ever since Mangor saw the strange stone, the site

had become sacred. He was scavenging, searching for roots and berries and fruit. Then it was there – announced by an unearthly wind. The obelisk, the standing stone. The sun shone round it, obscuring its shape and texture and colour.

But at the same time every hot season – at dawn when the sun was starting its longest journey across the sky at the height of summer – the stone returned. Every year. A sign, a message from the heavens. An inspiration.

What message was it bringing? The people of the plains didn't know. But they decided that this must be an important place, a sacred site. And so they brought their own stones – hewn from the living earth and dragged across the great grasses. They stood the stones in tribute, the intricate pattern the wise men devised lining up with the sunrise just as the strange stone that appeared every year did.

And finally there was one last stone to place. One day, it

would end. One year, the stone would not appear – and when that happened it would be time for the henge builders to erect their own massive stone in its place. A stone that echoed the shape and size of the stone that appeared, just as the other stones in the circle were designed to do.

The Doctor and Martha looked at the final picture in the sequence. The Doctor tapped his long index finger on the scanner, tracing the semicircle formed by the figures standing facing them. Almost as if they had been waiting for the TARDIS.

Some of the women were holding bundles of wild flowers. The men had their heads bowed.

'Any the wiser?' Martha asked.

The Doctor shook his head. 'Not really. It's been fun, but not that instructive.

I just hope,' he said quietly, 'that we haven't done anything, you know – silly.'

DOCTOR·WHO

OTHER GREAT FILES TO COLLECT

1 The Doctor

2 Rose

3 The Slitheen

4 The Sycorax

5 Mickey

6 K-9

7 The Daleks

8 The Cybermen

9 Martha

10 Captain Jack

11 The Cult of Skaro

12 The TARDIS